Anne of Green Gables
Anne grows up

L. M. Montgomery

About this Book

For the Student

🎧 Listen to all of the story and do some activities on your Audio CD
💬 Talk about the story

tune° When you see the orange dot you can check the word in the glossary

 Prepare for Cambridge English: Key (KET) for Schools

For the Teacher

 A state-of-the-art interactive learning environment with 1000s of free online self-correcting activities for your chosen readers.

Go to our Readers Resource site for information on using readers and downloadable Resource Sheets, photocopiable Worksheets and Answer Keys. Plus free sample tracks from the story.

www.helblingreaders.com

For lots of great ideas on using Graded Readers consult Reading Matters, the Teacher's Guide to using Helbling Readers.

Level 3 Structures

Present continuous for future	Cardinal / ordinal numbers
Present perfect	*One / ones*
Present perfect versus past simple	Reflexive pronouns
Should / shouldn't (advice and obligation)	Indefinite pronouns
Must / should	
Need to / have to	*Too* plus adjective
Will	*Not* plus adjective plus *enough*
Ever / never	Relative pronouns *who*, *which* and *that*
Would like	Prepositions of time, place and movement
So do I / neither do I	
Question tags	

Structures from lower levels are also included

	About the Author	6
	About the Book	7
	Before Reading	8
1	Anne's confession	13
2	A strange cake	19
3	Anne's new dress	22
4	Hair trouble	26
5	A boating accident	29
6	Anne prepares for Queen's	34
7	School starts again	38
8	The big exam	39
9	The concert	42
10	A Queen's girl	45
11	A dream come true	49
12	Death comes to Green Gables	52
13	A bend in the road	56
	After Reading	61

HELBLING DIGITAL

HELBLING e-zone is an inspiring new state-of-the-art, easy-to-use interactive learning environment.

The online self-correcting activities include:
- reading comprehension;
- listening comprehension;
- vocabulary;
- grammar;
- exam preparation.

▪ **TEACHERS** register free of charge to set up classes and assign individual and class homework sets. Results are provided automatically once the deadline has been reached and detailed reports on performance are available at a click.

▪ **STUDENTS** test their language skills in a stimulating interactive environment. All activities can be attempted as many times as necessary and full results and feedback are given as soon as the deadline has been reached. Single student access is also available.

FREE INTERACTIVE ONLINE TEACHING AND LEARNING MATERIALS

1000s of free online interactive activities now available for **HELBLING READERS** and your other favourite Helbling Languages publications.

www.helbling-ezone.com — ONLINE ACTIVITIES

blog.helblingreaders.com

NEW

Love reading and readers and can't wait to get your class interested? Have a class library and reading programme but not sure how to take it a step further? The Helbling Readers BLOG is the place for you.

The **Helbling Readers BLOG** will provide you with ideas on setting up and running a Book Club and tips on reading lessons **every week**.

- Book Club
- Worksheets
- Lesson Plans

Subscribe to our **BLOG** and you will never miss out on our updates.

About the Author

Lucy Maud Montgomery was born in Clifton, Prince Edward Island in Canada in 1874. She was an only child•. Montgomery's mother died when she was 21 months old. Then she lived with her grandparents. They lived on a farm that was the inspiration• for 'Green Gables'.

Montgomery was an imaginative child. She liked boys' activities like fishing, climbing trees and inventing scary• ghost stories. She started writing stories at nine years old. During her time at high school one of her poems was published•.

In 1894 Montgomery went to university. She continued writing and in 1895 she published her first short story, for the fee• of five dollars.

After university she worked as a teacher but then she left to become a journalist for a newspaper. She wrote her stories before and after work. It was difficult and she soon left the newspaper to write full time.

In 1904 Montgomery finished writing her first book, *Anne of Green Gables*. It was rejected• many times before it was published in 1908. *Anne of Green Gables* was translated into 20 languages.

In 1911 Montgomery married a minister•, Ewen Macdonald. They lived in Ontario with their children.

Lucy Maud Montgomery died at the age of 68 in Toronto.

Glossary

- **fee:** price; money you earn for a job
- **inspiration:** idea behind something
- **minister:** religious guide
- **only child:** with no brothers or sisters
- **published:** put in a newspaper or book
- **rejected:** said 'no' to
- **scary:** that make you afraid

About the Book

Anne of Green Gables – *Anne grows up* follows on from *Anne arrives*. It is set in Prince Edward Island in Canada in the late 1870s in a town called Avonlea. The novel follows the adventures of an 11-year-old orphan•, Anne.

The story begins when Anne is sent to Prince Edward Island after Matthew and Marilla Cuthbert decide to adopt• a boy from the orphanage to help Matthew on their farm. Through a mistake, the orphanage sends a girl, Anne. Matthew and Marilla take pity on• her and decide to adopt her.

Anne grows up to become a hard-working, kind and loving young woman. She learns to love school and studying, and dreams of becoming a teacher. She wants to get a good job but is also very close to her family and friends in Avonlea. At the beginning of the story Anne has to learn the difference between imagination and reality, how to forgive and not to be too vain•. But as Anne grows up, the themes in the story change, too, to include the importance of friendship, helping people and being hard-working.

Montgomery's Anne is a much-loved character and Mark Twain said Anne was 'the dearest and most moving• and delightful• child since the immortal Alice' (from *Alice's Adventures in Wonderland*).

The TV film *Anne of Green Gables* (1985) won lots of prizes and is a faithful adaptation of the book.

- **adopt:** take as their child
- **delightful:** lovely
- **moving:** making you feel emotion
- **orphan:** child with no living parents
- **take pity on:** feel sorry for
- **vain:** thinking about how you look

Before Reading

1 Listen and match the descriptions to the characters. Number the pictures 1 to 6.

A **Anne**

B **Gilbert**

C **Aunt Josephine**

D **Mr and Mrs Allan**

E **Matthew**

F **Mrs Rachel**

2 Listen again and complete the sentences with the correct name from Exercise 1.

1 Laughing was something .... did not do very often.
2 .... were a young couple full of enthusiasm and good intentions, and everyone in Avonlea liked them.
3 .... secretly wanted to be born in the days of King Arthur because they seemed so much more romantic than the present.
4 .... was her enemy. Last year he called her 'carrots' in front of the whole school. And she still hated him.
5 .... had heart problems. The doctor said that he needed to relax.
6 .... always knew everything about everyone in Avonlea.

Before Reading

3 Match the different jobs from the story with the correct definition.

a) ☐ shop assistant   b) ☐ church minister
c) ☐ Sunday school teacher   d) ☐ politician

1 person who teaches a religious class at church on a Sunday
2 person who serves you in a shop
3 person who helps govern a country or area
4 person who guides a religious community

4 Write the correct job under each picture. Use the jobs from Exercise 3.

....

....

....

....

5 Work with a friend. Ask and answer the questions about jobs.

a) Which of these jobs would you like to do and why?
b) Which of these jobs would you not like to do and why not?
c) What job would you like to do when you are older?
d) Do you need to study hard to do this job?
e) Why do you think it is important to study hard at school?

Before Reading

1 Match the words to the pictures.

> platform   boat   log   land   water   pond

K 2 Choose the best word to complete the sentences below.

a) The .... was floating in the water.
   1 pond   **2** log   **3** land

b) Gilbert came by in his ....
   1 boat   **2** platform   **3** land

c) They were standing on a wooden .... built out into the water.
   1 boat   **2** pond   **3** platform

d) The girls pushed the boat into the .... with Anne inside.
   1 boat   **2** pond   **3** platform

e) Gilbert came in a boat and bought me to ....
   1 land   **2** boat   **3** log

f) The boat started to fill with ....
   1 water   **2** land   **3** log

Before Reading

3 Match the words from the story with the correct definition.

a) ☐ academy   b) ☐ scholarship
c) ☐ teacher   d) ☐ exam
e) ☐ study   f) ☐ certificate

1 Money given to help a student study.
2 Place to train and learn things after you have finished school.
3 After passing a test or a course, you get this special piece of paper.
4 Person who helps you to learn something.
5 You usually do this alone, sometimes a lot before a test.
6 After studying something, you have this to test your knowledge.

4 Use the words from Exercise 3 to complete the sentences below.

a) When he passed the exam, Gilbert got a .... from the Academy.

b) Anne loved her .... , Miss Stacy, because she taught her a lot.

c) She finished school and went to the .... to get her Teacher's Certificate.

d) He had to .... a lot to be accepted into the Academy.

e) Most students are nervous before an ....

f) The .... was for one thousand dollars.

1 Anne's confession

Matthew and Marilla Cuthbert are brother and sister. They live together at Green Gables on Prince Edward Island, Canada, in a little town called Avonlea.

Last year they decided they wanted to adopt a boy from an orphanage• to help them on their farm. But instead of a boy, Anne Shirley, an eleven-year-old orphan• girl, arrived at Avonlea station. Matthew and Marilla soon began to like Anne's strange ways and affectionate• character so they decided to keep her. Over the following year Anne became best friends with a girl called Diana Barry but then sworn enemies• with a boy called Gilbert Blythe.

Here we meet up with Anne again for more adventures as she grows up.

Anne saw a flashing light• from her bedroom window and she ran down to the kitchen to speak to Marilla.

'Can I visit Diana?' Anne asked. 'Diana and I have invented a code•. We put a light in the window. Then we make flashes by passing paper in front of it. Five flashes means that something is very important.'

'Okay,' Marilla agreed. 'But be back in ten minutes.'

Glossary

- **affectionate:** loving
- **code:** secret language of signs or words
- **flashing light:** light that comes and goes
- **orphan:** child with no living parents
- **orphanage:** place where children without parents live
- **sworn enemies:** people who hate each other

13

Ten minutes later Anne rushed● back into the kitchen.

'Marilla,' Anne said quickly. 'Tomorrow is Diana's birthday. She's invited me to a concert, and then for a sleepover● at her house tomorrow night. Marilla, please let me go,' said Anne.

'No. I don't agree with little girls going to concerts.'

'But it's for a special reason. It's Diana's birthday. Her birthday only happens once a year. Please can I go, Marilla?' said Anne.

'No. Now go to bed. It's past eight.'

Anne went slowly and sadly up to bed.

The next day, however, Matthew persuaded Marilla to change her mind●. Anne could go to her first concert. It was great. Anne enjoyed everything at the concert, until Gilbert Blythe recited● a poem. Gilbert was her enemy. Last year he called her 'carrots' in front of the whole school. And she still hated him.

The house was dark when Anne and Diana got to the Barrys' house for the sleepover. The girls were sleeping in the spare● room near the living room.

'Let's run and see who gets to the bed first,' said Anne.

The girls quickly got changed into their night clothes. Then they ran and jumped on the bed in the spare room. Suddenly someone moved and spoke in the bed.

'Help!' a voice said.

Anne and Diana jumped off the bed.

Glossary

● **persuaded...mind:** made Marilla change her decision
● **recited:** said aloud

● **rushed:** went quickly
● **sleepover:** when children spend a night at another person's house
● **spare:** extra

They ran upstairs as fast as they could.

Anne was very afraid. 'What was that thing in the bed?' she asked.

'It was Aunt Josephine,' said Diana, laughing. 'She's father's aunt. She's very old, about seventy. I didn't know she was sleeping in that bed. She will be frightened and angry. But it was so funny!' said Diana, still laughing.

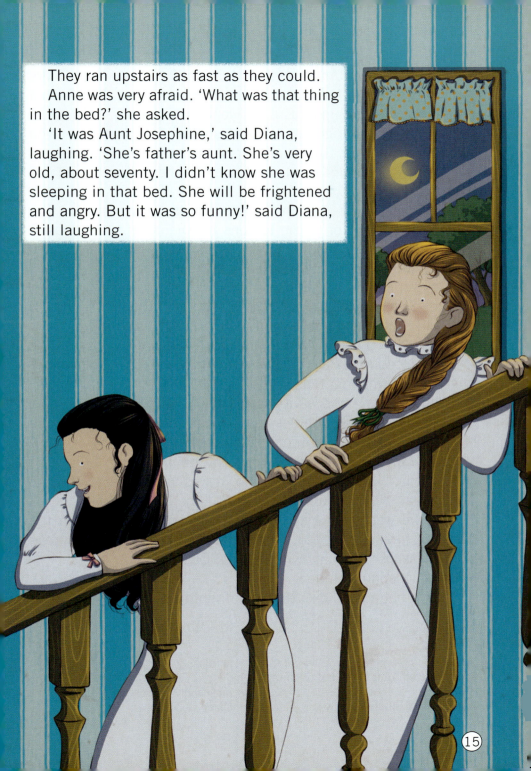

The next day when Anne went to visit Marilla's good friend, Mrs Rachel Lynde, she knew about Aunt Josephine, too. Mrs Rachel always knew everything about everyone in Avonlea.

'You and Diana frightened Aunt Josephine last night when you jumped on her bed. She's very angry now,' said Mrs Rachel.

'Oh, it was my idea to run and jump on the bed, not Diana's,' said Anne.

'Well, old Aunt Josephine now wants to go home. She promised• to pay for music lessons for Diana. But she doesn't want to now. The Barrys are very upset•,' said Mrs Rachel.

Anne went immediately to Diana's house.

'Was your Aunt Josephine very angry?' asked Anne.

'Yes. She says she wants to go home,' said Diana.

'Well, I'm going to tell her it was my fault•,' said Anne.

'Anne, don't!' said Diana. 'She's really angry.'

Miss Josephine Barry was knitting• by the fire. She looked angry. Anne was frightened.

'Who are you?' said Aunt Josephine.

'I'm Anne of Green Gables and I want to confess•,' said Anne.

'Confess what?' said Aunt Josephine.

'It was my fault last night. You can't punish Diana.'

'Oh, can't I? Diana jumped, too. It was very disrespectful• to jump on an old lady in her bed,' said Aunt Josephine.

'But we were only playing. We didn't know you were in the bed. We have apologized. Please forgive• Diana. Let her have music lessons. Be angry with me, not Diana.'

Aunt Josephine smiled.

'That's not a good excuse. I was frightened.'

Glossary

- **confess:** say you did something bad
- **disrepectful:** rude; not kind or caring
- **forgive:** not be angry with
- **it was my fault:** (here) it was my idea
- **knitting:**
- **promised:** said she will do it
- **upset:** worried; sad

Anne of Green Gables

'I'm sure you were frightened. I don't *know* but I can *imagine*. Do you have any imagination, Aunt Josephine? Think of Diana and me. Can you imagine our situation? We didn't know there was a person in the bed in the spare room. We thought the bed was empty when we jumped. So you can imagine we were very frightened when we heard your voice. We ran all the way upstairs and didn't sleep all night.'

Then Aunt Josephine laughed. Laughing was something Aunt Josephine did not do very often.

'Well,' Aunt Josephine said. 'I *imagine* you were frightened, too.'

'So, will you forgive Diana? Will you stay in Avonlea now?' asked Anne.

'Yes, I think I will. But you must come and talk to me sometimes,' said Aunt Josephine.

Aunt Josephine unpacked her bags and stayed in Avonlea for a month. Anne visited her often and they became good friends.

IMAGINE

What is the difference between 'know' and 'imagine'?
Do you think imagination is important?
Tell a friend.

2 A strange cake

Avonlea had a new minister• and a new Sunday school• teacher, Mr and Mrs Allan. They were a young couple full of enthusiasm and good intentions•, and everyone in Avonlea liked them. Anne wanted Mrs Allan to be her friend.

'Mrs Allan is lovely. She's a great teacher. She has a lovely smile. I wish• I had a lovely smile, Marilla,' said Anne.

'Mr and Mrs Allan have been everywhere for tea•. We must invite them for tea, too. We can invite them on Wednesday,' said Marilla.

'Marilla, can I make a cake for Mrs Allan?'

'Yes, you can,' said Marilla.

Monday and Tuesday were busy days at Green Gables. Marilla and Anne prepared lots of different food for the Allans' visit. They wanted the tea to be perfect. Anne was very excited.

On Wednesday morning Anne got up early to make the cake for Mrs Allan. She had a cold• and did not feel very well but she felt better after the cake went in the oven. Then Anne helped prepare the table for the tea.

The Allans arrived and everything went well. They all ate the different food and drank their tea. Matthew talked to the minister but he was too shy• to talk to Mrs Allan (Matthew was often shy talking to women). Then it was time for Anne's cake.

'No, no thank you,' said Mrs Allan. 'I'm very full•.'

Glossary

- **cold:** infection causing you to sneeze and to have a wet nose
- **full:** eaten lots
- **good intentions:** wanting to do good
- **minister:** (here) religious guide
- **shy:** afraid; timid
- **Sunday school:** a religion class at church on a Sunday
- **tea:** (here) light evening meal
- **wish:** when you really want something

'Mrs Allan, Anne made this special cake for you,' said Marilla.

'Then, I'll have a small piece,' said Mrs Allan.

Mrs Allan ate silently. Her face looked very strange. Then Marilla ate a piece.

'It's horrible. Mrs Allan, don't eat it. Anne, taste• it. What did you use?' asked Marilla.

'Only vanilla•,' said Anne.

She tasted her cake. Her face became red.

'Go and get the vanilla,' said Marilla.

Anne returned with a bottle. There was brown liquid in it. The label said, 'Best Vanilla'.

Marilla smelled• it.

'Oh, Anne, last week I broke a medicine bottle and so I put the medicine in this old vanilla bottle. I didn't tell you so it was my mistake, but why didn't you smell it?'

'I had such a bad cold. It was impossible to smell,' said Anne. And she turned and ran to her room.

CAKE

What happened to Anne's cake?
Has anything like this ever happened to you?
Tell a friend.

Glossary

- **smelled:** used her noise to sense a perfume, etc.
- **taste:** try to sense the substance with the mouth
- **vanilla:** sweet flavouring used for cakes and biscuits

Anne of Green Gables

Anne was crying on her bed when she heard someone walk into the room.

'Marilla, Mrs Allan will think I put poison• in the cake. But the medicine isn't poisonous. Please tell Mrs Allan,' said Anne.

'You can tell her now,' said a happy voice.

Anne turned and saw Mrs Allan smiling by her bed.

'Don't cry, dear little girl. It's a mistake. And everybody can make mistakes,' said Mrs Allan.

'I wanted to make a special cake for you, Mrs Allan,' said Anne.

'Yes, I know. Now, stop crying and show me your flower garden,' said Mrs Allan.

Anne and Mrs Allan went down to the garden together. Anne tried her best to forget about the cake. They had a lovely time and Anne found a new friend in the smiling Mrs Allan.

'Marilla,' said Anne when they were alone again. 'Isn't it nice thinking about tomorrow? It will be a new day with no mistakes in it.'

'Yes, but I know you'll make some more mistakes tomorrow,' said Marilla.

'But I never make the same mistake twice,' said Anne.

'Yes, because you always make new mistakes,' said Marilla.

'There must be a limit to the mistakes one person can make,' said Anne.

• **poison:** something you eat or drink that can kill you

3 Anne's new dress

Matthew was watching Anne and her friends. Anne was different from the other girls but he didn't know why. He was worried.

'Anne isn't dressed like the other girls. That's it!' he thought.

He decided that Anne needed a pretty dress. It was almost Christmas and a new dress was a perfect present.

The next day Matthew went to buy a dress for Anne. The shop assistant• was a very pretty young woman. Suddenly Matthew became very nervous• and shy.

'What can I do for you, Mr Cuthbert?' asked the woman.

'Do you… Have you any-any-any garden rakes•?' said Matthew.

'Yes,' said the woman, surprised. 'I'll go and get you one.'

When the woman came back Matthew tried again but this time he asked for brown-brown-brown sugar. The woman gave him sugar but she began to think that Matthew was crazy•!

Matthew went home with a rake and lots of brown sugar, but no dress for Anne.

The next day Matthew asked Mrs Rachel to help him.

'Of course I'll help you. I'll buy the material and I'll make it tomorrow. I know exactly what to make,' said Mrs Rachel.

'Can you make the sleeves• the new way?' asked Matthew.

'Puffy sleeves•?' said Mrs Rachel. 'Yes, I can.'

Marilla knew that Matthew was planning something. Then when Mrs Rachel arrived with the dress on Christmas Eve, she understood.

'Matthew, this will make Anne very vain•,' said Marilla. 'She will be happy but I think those sleeves are stupid.'

Glossary

- **crazy:** mad; strange
- **garden rakes:**

- **nervous:** not relaxed
- **puffy sleeves:**

- **shop assistant:** person who serves you in a shop
- **sleeves:** part of clothing that covers the arm
- **vain:** thinking about how you look

On Christmas morning Matthew gave Anne the dress.

Anne was silent. It was the most beautiful dress. She looked at the color, the ribbons• and the sleeves.

'Anne, this is a Christmas present for you. Don't you like it?' said Matthew.

Anne's eyes were full of tears.

'Like it? Matthew, it's perfect. Look at those sleeves! I think I am dreaming,' said Anne.

'You didn't need it but you must take care of it. Here's a ribbon for your hair, too. Now eat your breakfast,' said Marilla.

'I can't eat breakfast. Breakfast is too boring. Look at that dress! I'm so glad that puffy sleeves are still in fashion. I must be a very good girl. I really will try hard now.'

After breakfast Diana arrived.

'Merry Christmas, Diana. I have something amazing to show you. Matthew has given me the loveliest dress, with puffy sleeves,' said Anne.

'I've got something more for you. It's from Aunt Josephine,' said Diana.

Anne opened the present. She read the card, 'For the Anne-girl. Merry Christmas.'

There was a pair of very beautiful leather shoes.

'Diana, I think I am dreaming,' said Anne.

'Now you won't have to borrow• shoes for the school concert tonight,' said Diana.

Glossary

- **borrow:** (here) use someone else's shoes and then return them later
- **ribbons:**

Anne of Green Gables

The school concert that evening was a success. The little hall was crowded. Everyone was very good, but Anne was the star of the show.

Later, when Anne and Diana were walking home, Anne said, 'I was so nervous, Diana. I felt like a million eyes were looking at me. I didn't think I could begin. Then I thought of my lovely puffy sleeves and felt brave. I saw someone crying when I finished. I will remember that,' said Anne.

'Gilbert Blythe was amazing. You aren't kind to him, Anne. I saw Gilbert take a rose that fell from your hair. He put it in his pocket. You're so romantic, you must be pleased about that,' said Diana.

'I do not talk or think about that person, ever,' said Anne.

That night Marilla and Matthew sat talking after Anne went to bed. They were at the concert, too.

'I think our Anne did very well,' said Matthew.

'Yes, she did. And she looked good, too. I was proud of• Anne tonight. However, I'm not going to tell her,' said Marilla.

'I was proud of her and I told her before she went to bed. We must think about her future, Marilla. I think she'll need more than Avonlea school soon,' said Matthew.

'There's time to think about that. She's only thirteen in March. She's intelligent and we can send her to Queen's Academy•, in Charlottetown. Maybe in a year or two.'

'Well, we can think about it, Marilla,' said Matthew.

• **proud of:** pleased with

• **Queen's Academy:** place for training to be a teacher in the area

4 Hair trouble

It was April. Marilla was going home after a meeting. Anne was at home making dinner. Marilla loved coming home to Anne. She was thirteen now and she was really growing up.

Marilla walked into the kitchen. It was cold. There was no fire and no dinner. And there was no sign of Anne. Marilla was suddenly very angry.

'I'll fix• Anne,' thought Marilla. 'She shouldn't promise something and not do it. She's really in trouble•.'

When Matthew arrived and sat at the table, Marilla was cooking and talking about Anne.

'Maybe she can explain why she didn't do her chores•,' said Matthew.

'I think she'll find it hard to explain. Of course you'll agree with her. But I'm raising• her, not you.'

It was dark now and Anne still wasn't home. Marilla cleaned the kitchen angrily. She went to Anne's room to get something and she was surprised to find Anne lying in bed.

'Anne! Were you sleeping?'

'No,' said Anne.

'Are you sick?' asked Marilla.

Anne tried to hide in the bed.

'No. But please, Marilla, go away and don't look at me. I'm very sad. I don't care about school or choir•. I'm finished. Please, Marilla, go away,' said Anne.

'Anne Shirley, tell me what you've done.'

'Look at my hair, Marilla,' said Anne.

Glossary

- **choir:** organised group of singers
- **chores:** jobs around the house
- **fix:** (here) talk to
- **in trouble:** naughty
- **raising:** helping someone grow
- **traveling salesman:** person who travels and sells things
- **vanity:** thinking about how you look

Anne of Green Gables

Marilla looked carefully. Anne's hair was very strange.
'Anne Shirley, your hair is green!'
'Yes, it's green. I thought nothing was as bad as red hair. But now I know it's ten times worse to have green hair,' said Anne.
'You haven't done anything strange for more than two months. I was expecting something. What did you do?' said Marilla.
'I colored it,' said Anne.
'Anne that is very bad,' said Marilla.
'Yes, I knew it was a little bad. I thought it was better than red hair,' said Anne.
'But why did you color it green?' asked Marilla.
'Well, he said my hair was going to be black. He promised.'
'Who?' said Marilla.
'The traveling salesman• who was here this afternoon.'
'Anne Shirley, I told you never to let these people in the house,' said Marilla.
'I didn't. I went outside. He promised it was going to color my hair black. So I bought it. I used the whole bottle. Marilla, look at me. I'm very sorry,' said Anne.
'Well, this is what vanity• does, Anne. Let's wash your hair first,' said Marilla.

The color didn't change.

'People have forgotten my other mistakes, like the medicine in the cake. But they'll never forget this. I am the unhappiest girl in Avonlea,' said Anne.

Anne stayed inside for a week and hid from everyone. Well, apart from Marilla, Matthew and Diana. She washed her hair every day. At the end of the week Marilla made a decision.

'Anne, we must cut your hair,' said Marilla.

Anne wanted to cry. But she knew Marilla was right. She got the scissors.

'Please cut it. I'm going to cry but do it,' said Anne.

Later she went to her room and looked in the mirror. She was not pretty. She turned the mirror to the wall.

'I'll never look at myself again until my hair grows,' said Anne.

Suddenly she turned the mirror again.

'Yes, I will. I'll look at my hair every day. That's my punishment.'

Anne went back to school. Anne's very short hair got lots of attention. But her classmates never knew the real reason.

APPEARANCE

Have you ever done something to change your appearance?
How did it make you feel? Tick (✓).
- ☐ better   ☐ worse

🕪 Tell a friend.

5 A boating accident

It was Anne's idea that they dramatize 'Elaine•'. They were studying Tennyson's poem in school and Elaine and Lancelot and Guinevere and King Arthur• had become very real people to them. Anne secretly wanted to be born in those days because they seemed so much more romantic than the present.

Anne, Diana, Ruby and Jane were standing by the pond•, in Avonlea, on a small wooden platform• built out into the water.

'Well, I'll be Elaine. Diana, you can wrap• me in a shawl•. Then I can float on the pond in the boat. It will be very romantic.'

Anne was lying in the boat with her hands across her heart. The shawl was around her shoulders. Her eyes were closed.

Glossary

- **Elaine:** poem by Alfred Lord Tennyson called 'Lancelot and Elaine'
- **Elaine… King Arthur:** characters from the poem
- **platform:** (here) raised area above the water
- **pond:** small lake; area of water
- **shawl:** large scarf used to cover shoulders
- **wrap:** cover

29

'She really looks dead. I feel frightened, girls. Is it okay to do this?' said Ruby, nervously.

'Ruby, don't talk, concentrate!' said Anne. 'I can't talk because I'm dead. Jane, organize things.'

Jane followed Anne's orders and prepared Elaine for the scene.

'Now, she's ready. Anne, you smile. The poem says you are smiling. That's better. Now push the boat,' said Jane.

The boat started moving quickly. The girls ran off to meet Anne further down the pond. They were very excited.

For a few minutes Anne enjoyed the boat ride. Then the boat started to fill with water. Anne was in danger. She screamed• but nobody heard. She saw a log• and jumped into the water to hold on to it.

Ruby, Jane and Diana were waiting further down the pond on the next platform. Then they saw the boat sink•. They were sure that Anne was in it. They screamed and ran further up the pond to the boat.

From the water Anne saw them running. She held on to the log. She was very uncomfortable but she was sure that the girls were coming to save her.

Minutes passed. It seemed like hours. Where were the girls? She imagined lots of terrible things.

Then, Gilbert Blythe came by in another boat.

Gilbert saw Anne. She looked angrily at him as she held on to the log.

'Anne Shirley! How did you get there?' asked Gilbert.

He didn't wait for an answer. He pulled her into the boat. She was very angry and very wet.

Glossary

• **log:** big piece of wood

• **screamed:** shouted; cried
• **sink:** go under the water

'What happened?' asked Gilbert.

Anne wanted to get away from Gilbert as soon as possible.

'Take me to land•,' she said, without looking at him.

He took her to land. Anne thanked him very coldly. She wanted to run away quickly.

'Anne, can't we be friends? I'm really sorry I joked• about your hair. I think your hair is very pretty now. Let's be friends.'

Anne thought but then remembered everything. Gilbert called her 'carrots' in front of the whole school. No, she hated Gilbert, for life.

'No, I'll never be friends with you, Gilbert Blythe,' she said.

'I'll never ask you to be friends again, Anne Shirley,' said Gilbert, angrily.

Gilbert quickly left in his boat. Anne walked up the path. She was trying to feel good but she felt sad. Did she say the wrong thing to Gilbert?

Walking back she met Jane and Diana. They were very happy to see her, 'Anne, we thought you were dead. It was our fault.'

'Anne, how did you escape?' asked Diana.

'I held on to a log. Then Gilbert came in a boat and brought me to land,' said Anne.

'Anne, it's so romantic. So, you're friends again, aren't you?' said Jane.

'No. I don't want to ever hear the word "romantic" again, Jane Andrews. I'm very sorry you were so scared, girls. It's all my fault.'

Glossary

- **joked:** said something to make people laugh
- **land:** earth; place that is not water

Anne of Green Gables

Later Mr and Mrs Barry and the Cuthberts heard what happened. There was a lot of trouble for Anne and the girls.

'Will you ever stop making mistakes, Anne?' asked Marilla.

'Yes, I think I've learned a valuable lesson today. I know I've made lots of mistakes but each one taught me something. The medicine cake mistake taught me about cooking carefully. Coloring my hair taught me about vanity. And now I've learnt not to be romantic. It is useless in Avonlea,' said Anne.

But Matthew put a hand on Anne's shoulder after Marilla left.

'Don't give up all your romance, Anne. A little is a good thing.'

ROMANCE

Are you romantic?

Think of something romantic to do or say to someone you like.

Write them on pieces of paper then put them in a bag.

Take turns to read aloud.

Discuss in small groups.

6 Anne prepares for Queen's

Anne was dreaming in front of the fire. Marilla looked over at her and smiled. Anne had no idea how much Marilla loved her.

'Anne, Miss Stacy was here this afternoon when you were with Diana.'

Anne jumped at Marilla's voice.

'I'm in trouble. I wanted to tell you. I was reading a novel at lunch time yesterday. I wanted to finish it so I continued reading in class. I was so ashamed•. I cried so much and asked Miss Stacy to forgive me. But she said she forgave me. It was wrong of her to tell you.'

'Well, you don't want to hear what Miss Stacy said. You're more interested in talking,' said Marilla.

'Oh! Please tell me, Marilla.'

'Miss Stacy wants to organize a class for students to study for the entrance exam into Queen's Academy. So Anne, do you want to study to become a teacher?' asked Marilla.

'That's my dream. Well, for the last six months. A teacher. But is it expensive?' asked Anne.

'Don't worry about that. Matthew and I want to give you a good education. You can get married but you must have a career. You can join the Queen's class, Anne.'

'Marilla, thank you. I'm so grateful• to you and Matthew. And I'll work very hard. Don't expect much in geometry, but with hard work I can do well in the other subjects,' said Anne.

'Miss Stacy says you are bright• and hard-working,' said Marilla.

Glossary

- **ashamed:** not proud or happy
- **bright:** clever; intelligent
- **grateful:** full of thanks

Anne of Green Gables

Miss Stacy said a lot more but Marilla didn't tell Anne. She thought Anne was already too vain.

'You have eighteen months before the entrance exam. You can start soon but be calm•, Miss Stacy says.'

'I'll study harder now. Imagine me being a teacher like Miss Stacy,' said Anne.

Soon the Queen's class was ready. Gilbert, Anne and five other students joined it. Diana didn't. This was a disaster for Anne. She was always with Diana. The first afternoon of extra lessons, Anne wanted to cry. She watched Diana leave the school room.

'Marilla, I felt so sad,' said Anne to Marilla later. 'But I think the class is going to be very interesting. We all have different ambitions• – a teacher, a politician and even a minister.'

'What's Gilbert's ambition?' asked Marilla.

'I don't know,' said Anne, coldly.

The two of them were open rivals• in school now. After the day on the pond Gilbert ignored Anne. She said he wasn't important in her life, but in reality she thought that he was. Anne realized too late that she was wrong not to forgive him.

> ## RIVALS
> Do you have a rival at school, or in sport?
> Do you think it is good or bad to have rivals?
> Tell a friend.

- **ambitions:** things you want to do or become
- **calm:** not nervous; peaceful
- **rivals:** two people competing against each other, both wanting to be the best

The winter was spent going to school and choir practice and studying for the exam. Soon it was summer vacation time.

'You've done good work this past year. Now have a good vacation. Be ready for next year. The last year before the entrance exam will be difficult,' said Miss Stacy.

When she got home, Anne put her school books away.

'I'm not going to look at a school book on vacation. I want to let my imagination run wild for the summer. Maybe this is my last summer as a young girl.'

The next day Mrs Rachel came to Green Gables. Marilla missed a town meeting earlier that week. Mrs Rachel knew something was wrong.

'Matthew had heart problems. But he's all right now. The doctor says he needs to relax and and not work so hard. That is almost impossible,' said Marilla.

Mrs Rachel and Marilla sat in the living room. Anne made tea and biscuits.

'Anne is a good girl. Does she help you a lot?' asked Mrs Rachel.

'She is a good girl and she's reliable•. Her imagination was a problem, but I trust her completely now,' said Marilla.

'She's been here now for three years. I was worried the first time I met her. But I was wrong and now I think she is wonderful. She's very pretty now, too,' said Mrs Rachel.

Glossary

• **reliable:** does what she says she will do

7 School starts again

Anne enjoyed the next year at school and worked hard during lessons. As the year passed she also became much quieter than before.

'You don't talk as much as before, Anne. You don't use as many big words. What's happened?' asked Marilla.

Anne seemed embarrassed.

'I don't want to talk as much. I like thinking. Now I'm almost grown up, I don't want to use big words. It's fun to be almost grown up, but there's so much to learn. There isn't any time for big words. Miss Stacy says we must write all our essays as simply as possible. It was difficult at first. But now I see it's so much better,' said Anne.

'You've only got two months before the entrance exam. Will you pass?' asked Marilla.

'I don't know. Do you think I've studied enough? We're going to have practice exams in June. I wish they were finished. Sometimes I wake up at night and think about it. What happens to people who fail?' asked Anne.

'They go to school next year and try again,' said Marilla.

'Oh, no. I can't fail. Imagine: the others, including Gilbert, all pass and then I fail? How terrible. And I get so nervous in exams. I wish I was calm,' said Anne.

Anne put her head back into her book. She continued thinking about her life and the exam. She was very worried.

WORRIES

Do you ever worry about things?
Tell a friend.

8 The big exam

It was the end of June and school was finished.

'It seems like the end of everything, doesn't it?' said Diana. She started crying.

'Stop it or I'll cry again. I don't think I will pass this exam,' said Anne.

'Yes, you will. I want to go with you. Imagine how much fun it will be.'

'Yes, but I will have to study a lot. It was so nice of your Aunt Josephine to ask me to stay at her house,' said Anne.

'You'll write to me, won't you?' asked Diana.

Anne went to Aunt Josephine's house on Monday.

On Wednesday Diana went to the post office.

There was a letter from Anne.

Dear Diana,

It's Tuesday night and I'm writing this from Aunt Josephine's house. Last night I was really lonely in my room without you.

This morning I went to the Academy. There were lots of students. People were doing funny things before the exam. One boy was talking to himself!

Then we went into the exam. Some of the girls looked so relaxed. My heart was beating so quickly. Then we did the English exam. Diana, I felt like I did four years ago when I asked Marilla about staying at Green Gables. In the afternoon we had a history exam. I think I did OK. But Diana, tomorrow we have geometry. I am worried about that.

Yours,

Anne

The exams finished and Anne went home on Friday evening. She was very tired but happy. Diana was waiting.

'It's wonderful to see you. I missed you. Did you do well?' asked Diana.

'I think so, except with geometry. I don't think I passed. It's so good to be back. Green Gables is the best place in the world,' said Anne.

'When do you get the results•?' asked Diana.

'In two weeks. They'll be in the newspaper. Two weeks of waiting,' said Anne.

'You'll pass. Don't worry.'

'I want to pass with a high score• or not at all,' said Anne. She seemed angry.

Diana understood that Anne wanted a higher score than Gilbert.

Anne and Gilbert were in competition with each other. They saw each other but didn't speak. It was like they were strangers•. Anne secretly wished that she was friends with Gilbert again. But she also wanted to get a higher score than him in the exam. Everyone thought Gilbert was going to get the highest score. She wanted to make Matthew and Marilla proud. Well, mostly Matthew.

The results were late. Finally after three weeks of waiting, they arrived. Diana came running to the house with a newspaper.

'Anne, you've passed. You and Gilbert. You're equal firsts•.' said Diana.

Anne took the newspaper. Yes, their names were at the top of a list of two hundred pupils. Wow!

'Look, everyone from Avonlea passed. Anne, your name is at the top of the list. Why are you so calm?' asked Diana.

Glossary

- **equal firsts:** they both have first place
- **results:** final mark in the exam
- **score:** mark; number
- **speechless:** unable to speak
- **were strangers:** didn't know each other

'I'm speechless•. I never dreamed of this. Wait, yes I did, well, once. I must tell Matthew right now,' said Anne.

They ran outside. Matthew was working and Mrs Rachel was talking to Marilla.

'Matthew, I've passed. I'm first. Well, one of the first,' said Anne.

'I knew it,' said Matthew. He looked at the newspaper.

'You've done well, Anne,' said Marilla.

'She has done well, Marilla,' said Mrs Rachel. Then she turned to Anne.

'Anne, we're all proud of you,' said Mrs Rachel.

That night Anne said a prayer of thanks and slept happily, thinking of the future.

9 The concert

Anne and Diana were getting ready for a concert. Anne was one of the performers•.

'There's something so stylish about you, Anne,' said Diana.

'And you have such a beautiful smile,' Anne replied.

'Are you nervous?' asked Diana.

'Not at all. I've spoken lots in public now. I'm reciting a poem that is very emotional.'

'Have you prepared yourself for an encore•?'

'They won't dream of encoring me. Come on, let's go.'

The girls went downstairs. Marilla was proud of how lovely Anne looked. But she didn't tell her.

At the hotel, Anne went to the performers' dressing room. She suddenly felt shy. The other performers were from the city. She was from the country.

Unfortunately, a professional speaker recited a poem before Anne. The audience• was captivated•. When it was time Anne walked slowly onto the stage•. But she had an attack of stage fright• and it paralyzed her completely. She stood without speaking. Then, she saw Gilbert in the audience. Anne thought that he was laughing at her.

Actually, Gilbert was smiling because he was enjoying the evening. He thought Anne looked beautiful.

Anne did not want to fail in front of Gilbert. Her nervousness vanished•. She began her poem. She was confident.

Glossary

- **audience:** people watching a concert
- **captivated:** very interested
- **encore:** repeat performance
- **performers:** people presenting something to the audience
- **stage:** area where people perform
- **stage fright:** feeling of fear at being in front of an audience
- **vanished:** went away

When Anne finished there was lots of applause•. She felt shy as she walked back to her seat. A lady from the city spoke to her.

'That was wonderful. They're encoring you. Go!' said the lady.

Anne went back on stage and recited another poem.

After the concert, the lady from the city introduced Anne to everybody. A tall girl paid her a compliment•. They had dinner in an elegant dining room. Diana and Jane were invited, too. Anne felt very pleased with the evening.

'What an evening! Anne, your poem was great. I was worried at first. You were better than that professional woman,' said Jane.

'No, I wasn't better than her. I'm only a schoolgirl, with a little talent. But I'm quite pleased that people liked my performance,' said Anne.

'Did you see all the diamonds• on those ladies? They were beautiful. Imagine being rich!' said Jane.

'We are rich. We're sixteen years old. We're happy and we've got imaginations. Look at that sky. It's not lovelier with money. Do you want to be that tall girl and look sad all your life? Or the lady from the city. She is nice but she's fat. You know you don't, Jane Andrews,' said Anne.

'I don't know. I think diamonds make you feel quite good,' said Jane.

'Well, I don't want to be anyone but myself. I'm quite happy to be Anne of Green Gables, with my pearl necklace• from Matthew.'

Glossary

- **applause:** when people clap after a concert
- **diamonds:**
- **paid her a compliment:** said something nice about her
- **pearl necklace:**

10 A Queen's girl

One evening Anne recited her poem at home for Marilla and Matthew. Marilla watched Anne. She remembered a frightened child with an ugly dress who arrived by mistake. Marilla started to cry.

'My poem has made you cry. That's good,' said Anne.

'No, I was feeling sad about how you've changed. You've grown up now and you're leaving. You look so stylish and tall in that dress,' said Marilla.

'Marilla! I haven't changed. I'm a little more elegant. But the real me is exactly the same. Remember that I'm always your little Anne. I will love you, Matthew and Green Gables forever,' said Anne.

Marilla loved how Anne used her words. She hugged° Anne.

Matthew was about to cry, too. He walked outside quietly.

'Well,' Matthew thought to himself. 'Anne's not spoilt°, she's intelligent and pretty, and loving. That's the most important. What a lucky mistake. It was fate°, Marilla and I needed Anne in our lives.'

When it was time for Anne to leave. Matthew took her to town. Marilla did lots of unnecessary housework work all day. But that night, when Marilla went to bed, she cried.

• **fate:** destiny; outside power controlling all events
• **hugged:** put her arms around with affection

• **spoilt:** having a bad character because people allow you to do what you want

45

Anne of Green Gables

Anne's first day at the Academy was very exciting. Anne met lots of new students and professors and received her timetable• for classes. Anne and Gilbert were following the same study path•. They were studying two years in one. They were getting their Teacher's Certificate• quicker. There were fifty students in her class but Anne felt lonely. She didn't have any friends. At least Gilbert was in her class. That made her happy. She had someone to compete against.

'Gilbert looks very hard working. Who will be my friend in this class? I can't have another best friend but I can have second-best friends. But these girls probably don't want to be friends with me,' thought Anne.

Later in her new bedroom, Anne felt even lonelier. She was staying in a boarding house• near Queen's Academy. It was nice but she was homesick•. She thought about her home at Green Gables. Outside the window was a street and lots of telephone wires• blocking the sky. She wanted to cry.

'I won't cry. I must imagine something funny,' said Anne.

Suddenly, a girl from home appeared. Anne forgot they weren't friends in Avonlea.

'I'm so glad you came,' said Anne.

'You were crying. You're homesick. I'm not homesick. This town's too exciting after old Avonlea. You shouldn't cry, Anne. It makes you all red. Do you have any cake from Marilla? That's why I came,' said the girl.

Glossary

- **boarding house:** place for students to stay and sleep while studying away from home
- **following...path:** studying the same subjects
- **homesick:** sad to be away from home
- **Teacher's Certificate:** qualification needed to become a teacher
- **telephone wires:**
- **timetable:** list of times

Jane and Ruby also came to visit Anne.

'I should study but I'm too excited. Anne, were you crying? I was crying, too. Then Ruby came and I stopped. Cake? Yum! From Avonlea, too,' said Jane.

The girls talked about their different study paths.

'Tomorrow there's an announcement• at school. There will be one scholarship• at Queen's.'

Anne thought of a new ambition. A Teacher's Certificate was good, but a scholarship was much better. She saw herself winning the scholarship, going to college• and graduating•. The scholarship was for the student with the highest score in English Literature. It was one thousand dollars for college fees•. Anne went to bed very excited that night.

'I'll win that scholarship. I can do it. Matthew will be proud. Imagine getting a Bachelor of Arts degree•! Life is so interesting with so many ambitions.'

STUDY PATH
What study path do you think you will take?
Ask and tell a friend.

Glossary

- **announcement:** public statement
- **Bachelor of Arts degree:** university or college qualification
- **college:** (here) university
- **fees:** price for attending
- **graduating:** successfully completing an academic course
- **scholarship:** money given to help a student study; (here) to have the money to go to college

11 A dream come true

At the end of the year after the exams, Anne and Jane were waiting for their results. Anne was quiet. She was nervous about the scholarship.

They walked to the entrance of Queen's. Some boys were carrying Gilbert on their shoulders. They were shouting, 'Hurrah for Gilbert. First place•!'

For a moment Anne felt disappointed•. She didn't want to disappoint Matthew.

Then suddenly, more shouting, 'Congratulations, Anne. You're the winner of the scholarship.'

The award ceremony• was held in the big assembly hall at the Academy. Matthew and Marilla sat in the audience. They watched Anne get her scholarship.

'Aren't you glad we kept her, Marilla?' said Matthew.

'It's not the first time I've been glad,' said Marilla.

WINNERS
Who won what?
Complete.
Anne ....
Gilbert ....

• **award ceremony:** public meeting when prizes are given

• **disappointed:** sad
• **place:** position in a competition or exam

Anne went home with Matthew and Marilla. Diana was waiting for her. Anne was very happy to be home.

'Diana, it's so good to be back. It's so good to see the trees and the flowers. And it's so good to see you again,' said Anne.

'You've done so well, Anne. I suppose you won't teach now because you have the scholarship.'

'No. I'm going to college in September,' said Anne.

'Gilbert is going to teach. He must. His father can't afford to send him to college next year. I think he'll teach here in Avonlea,' said Diana.

Anne was shocked•. She expected Gilbert to go to college, too. She felt very strange without Gilbert's competition.

The next morning at breakfast, Anne saw that Matthew did not look well. She waited for Matthew to go outside.

'Marilla, is Matthew okay?'

'No, he isn't. He's had some problems with his heart. But he's been a little better lately. Maybe now that you're home he will get better. You always make him happy,' said Marilla.

Anne took Marilla's face in her hands.

'You're looking tired, too. You work too hard. You must rest, now that I'm home. I'm going to take one day to visit all my favourite places. Then you can be lazy while I work,' said Anne.

Marilla smiled at Anne.

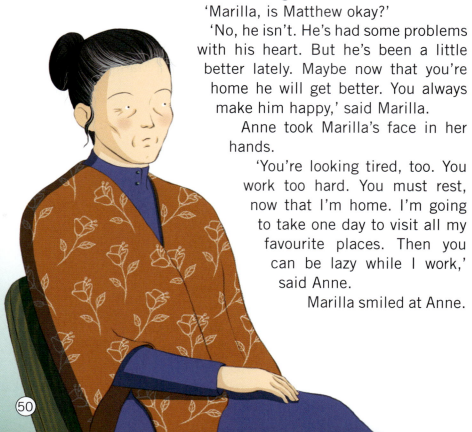

Anne of Green Gables

'Anne, it's not the work,' said Marilla. 'I have terrible headaches• because of my eyes. I can't read or sew• now. Well, Anne, you've done really well at Queen's. To get the Teacher's Certificate in one year and win the scholarship. Did you hear about the bank?'

'I heard it was in trouble. Why?' said Anne.

'Matthew is very worried. All our money is there. I wanted Matthew to put it in another bank. But Matthew knows the manager and he trusts• him,' said Marilla. She was worried.

Anne had a great day outside. She went everywhere. She ended her day talking to Matthew.

'You work too hard, Matthew. Please slow down,' said Anne.

'I can't. I'm getting old, Anne. And I forget that my body isn't as young as it was. I'm okay,' said Matthew.

'I wish I was a boy,' said Anne.

'Well, I think you're better than a dozen• boys, Anne. A boy didn't get the scholarship, did he? It was my girl. I'm so proud of you,' said Matthew.

Anne went to her room that night and sat at her open window. She was thinking about the past and dreaming about the future. It was the last night before sorrow• touched her life.

Glossary

- **a dozen:** twelve
- **headaches:** pains in the head
- **sew:**
- **shocked:** surprised
- **sorrow:** great sadness
- **trusts:** believes in

51

12 Death comes to Green Gables

'Matthew, are you sick?' asked Marilla.

Matthew's face was grey. He was holding a piece of paper. He fell to the ground.

'Anne, get help.'

Soon Mr and Mrs Barry and Mrs Rachel came. Mrs Rachel listened to Matthew's heart. She looked at Anne and Marilla sadly.

'Oh, Marilla. It's too late,' said Mrs Rachel.

'Mrs Rachel, you don't think Matthew is...' said Anne.

'I'm sorry, Anne. Yes,' said Mrs Rachel. She spoke quietly and sadly.

The doctor came and said that Matthew's death was quick. He thought shock was the reason. The shock was that the bank closed. All Matthew and Marilla's money was gone.

Soon lots of people came to give their condolences•.

Mr and Mrs Barry and Mrs Rachel stayed at Green Gables that night. But Anne wanted to be alone with her grief• so she went to her room. She tried to cry, but no tears fell.

In the middle of the night she woke up. She saw Matthew's face smiling at her. She heard his voice saying, 'My girl. I'm so proud of you.' Then she started crying. Marilla went to her.

'Ah Anne, shhhh. He was such a good brother to me. And he loved you so much,' said Marilla.

Two days later, they had Matthew's funeral•.

Glossary

- **condolences:** expressions of sympathy
- **funeral:** ceremony in which a dead person is buried or cremated
- **grief:** sadness

A few weeks later, Anne was talking to Mrs Allan. She felt guilty• when she enjoyed something.

'I miss him so much. Today Diana said something funny and I started laughing. I thought I wasn't ever going to laugh again,' said Anne.

'I can understand you. We feel like it's wrong to be interested in life again,' said Mrs Allan.

'I was at Matthew's grave• this afternoon. I felt good planting a rose. I was doing something that he liked. I hope he has roses like that in heaven. I must go home now. Marilla is alone.'

Anne walked slowly back home. Marilla was sitting outside. Anne sat beside her.

'Doctor Spencer was here. I have an eye test tomorrow. Will you be okay here alone? There's ironing and baking to do,' said Marilla.

'I will be fine. Diana is coming. Don't worry about me putting medicine in the cake or anything stupid,' said Anne.

Marilla laughed.

'You did make some silly mistakes, didn't you? Do you remember the time you colored your hair?'

'Yes, I laugh sometimes when I think about how much I worried about my hair. But I don't laugh much, because it was a big problem. I suffered a lot because of my hair and my freckles•.'

Glossary

- **freckles:** small brown spots of colour on your skin
- **grave:** place where a person is buried
- **guilty:** bad

Anne of Green Gables

'Anne, is Gilbert going to teach?' asked Marilla.

'Yes,' said Anne.

'He is a handsome boy. He looks like his father at that age. I was friends with Gilbert's father. I called him my boyfriend,' said Marilla.

Suddenly Anne was very interested in the conversation.

'What happened?' asked Anne.

'We had a fight. I didn't forgive him. I wanted to but I was angry. Then he left. I've always regretted• that. It was all forgotten. But I saw Gilbert last Sunday and I remembered everything,' said Marilla.

REGRET
Do you have something you regret doing?
Ask and tell a friend.

• **regretted:** been sorry I did

13 A bend in the road

Marilla's news from her visit to the doctor was not good. He told Marilla that she had to be very careful or she could go blind• in six months. Marilla knew she had to make some changes.

'Who was that man you were talking to before, Marilla?' asked Anne, a few days later.

'That was Mr Sadler. He wants to buy Green Gables.'

'No, you can't sell our home,' said Anne.

'I have to, I can't stay here alone. And I'm going blind,' said Marilla.

'Well, I'm not taking the scholarship. I've decided. Let me tell you my plans. Mr Barry is going to rent• the farm. I'm going to teach at the Carmody school. It's all organized. We'll be really happy here,' said Anne.

'But what about all your ambitions?' asked Marilla.

'I still have ambitions. I'm going to be a good teacher and I'm going to save your eyes. Also, I'm going to do a distance college course•. After Queen's my future seemed like it was a straight road. Now there is a bend•. I don't know what's around the bend, but I believe that it's good. I am sixteen and a half. I've decided,' said Anne. She was laughing now.

'You lovely girl. You've given me new life. I'll make it up to• you, Anne.'

Many people talked about Anne's change of plans. Nobody except Mrs Allan understood. Mrs Rachel was happy about Anne's change of plans, too.

Glossary

- **bend:** curve; (here) change in direction
- **blind**: not being able to see
- **distance college course:** follow the college course from home
- **make it up to:** do something to show appreciation
- **rent:** give a regular payment for the use of

Anne of Green Gables

Mrs Rachel came to visit one evening. Anne and Marilla were sitting outside.

'Well, Anne, I hear you've decided against college. I was very glad to hear that. I don't believe in girls going to college,' said Mrs Rachel.

'But I'm going to do my college course by distance, here at Green Gables. I'll study everything the same as college. I'll have lots of spare time, and I don't really want a professional position. I'm going to teach in Carmody,' said Anne.

'No, you're going to teach here in Avonlea,' said Mrs Rachel.

'No, Gilbert Blythe is teaching there.'

'Well, Gilbert heard about your situation. He suggested that you take the position. He's going to teach at White Sands. He knew that you wanted to stay with Marilla. I'm so pleased,' said Mrs Rachel.

'I don't think Gilbert should do this for me.'

'Nonsense. It's all organized. Take the job. What does all the flashing from the Barry house mean?' said Mrs Rachel.

'Diana is sending me a message. It's our old code. I have to go and see what she wants. Excuse me.'

Anne ran to Diana's house. Mrs Rachel watched her run.

'She's still a child,' said Mrs Rachel.

'In other ways, she's a woman,' said Marilla.

ANNE GROWS UP

In what ways has Anne grown up?
Work with a friend and make a list.

Anne of Green Gables

Later, Anne took fresh flowers to Matthew's grave. She met Gilbert as she was walking home.

'Gilbert. Thank you for what you did for me. I am very grateful,' said Anne, offering her hand to Gilbert.

Gilbert took her hand immediately.

'I was happy to do something for you. Now, can you forgive me?' asked Gilbert.

Anne laughed.

'I forgave you that day, but I didn't know it. I was so stubborn•,' said Anne.

'We will be best friends,' said Gilbert, still holding Anne's hand. 'This is fate. And we can really help each other. You're going to continue studying, aren't you? So am I. I'm going to walk home with you.'

Marilla was in the kitchen and Anne walked in.

'I didn't think you and Gilbert were friends. You were talking to him for thirty minutes,' said Marilla. She was smiling.

'We're friends now. Hmmm, half an hour? It seemed like a few minutes. But, we have years to catch up on•, Marilla,' said Anne.

- **catch up on:** talk about
- **stubborn:** not wanting to change my mind; proud

That night Anne sat at her window feeling very happy.

Her plans for the future changed after the first night home from Queen's Academy. But her new plans were as good. She had a job, ambition and true friendship. And there was always a bend in the road.

After Reading

Personal Response

1 Read each sentence. Which number is most true for you? Circle the number.

1 = Not really   **5 =** Definitely

a) I liked the story.

1   2   3   4   5

b) The story was easy to understand.

1   2   3   4   5

c) The story taught me new words and new expressions.

1   2   3   4   5

d) I think the story was for people of my age.

1   2   3   4   5

e) I want tell a friend to read this story.

1   2   3   4   5

2 Which characters did you like in the story? Why?

3 Has Anne changed by the end of this story? How?

4 What did Anne learn?

5 What was your favourite part of the story?

6 What did you learn from the story? Tick (✓).

a) ☐ Being stubborn isn't good for anyone.

b) ☐ Making mistakes is okay when you learn from them.

c) ☐ Fashion and the colour of your hair are really important.

d) ☐ It's important to care about yourself and other people.

After Reading

Comprehension

1 Are the following sentences true (T) or false (F)? Tick (✓).

		T	F
a)	Anne was 11 at the start of this story.	☐	☐
b)	Diana had a rich aunt called Josephine.	☐	☐
c)	Anne really admired Mrs Allan.	☐	☐
d)	Gilbert was sorry he called Anne 'carrots'.	☐	☐
e)	Marilla tried to poison Mrs Allan.	☐	☐
f)	Matthew bought Anne a new coat.	☐	☐
g)	Anne coloured her hair green because she liked the colour.	☐	☐
h)	It was Diana's idea to push Anne down the river in the boat.	☐	☐
i)	The boat began to sink with Anne in it.	☐	☐
j)	Gilbert got a higher score than Anne in the final exam.	☐	☐
k)	Anne had stage fright just before she went onto the stage.	☐	☐
l)	Anne and Gilbert went to Queens College.	☐	☐
m)	They both wanted to be teachers.	☐	☐
n)	Matthew died before Anne graduated from college.	☐	☐
o)	Marilla had a romantic relationship with Gilbert's father a long time ago.	☐	☐

2 Correct the false sentences in Exercise 1.

After Reading

3 Match the sentence halves to make complete sentences.

a) ☐ Avonlea had a new minister – he
b) ☐ Mrs Allan was a Sunday
c) ☐ The man promised the bottle was going
d) ☐ Anne wanted to get away from Gilbert as
e) ☐ Matthew went home with a
f) ☐ Gilbert was smiling because he

1 school teacher – she taught religion.
2 to colour Anne's hair black.
3 soon as possible.
4 rake and lots of brown sugar, but no dress.
5 was enjoying the evening.
6 was a religious guide.

4 Match 4 sentences from Exercise 3 with these pictures.

After Reading

Characters

1 Match the descriptions to the characters.

Anne

Diana

Aunt Josephine

Matthew

Gilbert

Mrs Allan

a) He studies hard. He has a boat. He is sorry about something.
b) She has lots of money. She doesn't often laugh. She is old.
c) He works hard on the farm. He is shy of women.
d) She makes lots of mistakes. She has an affectionate character. She has red hair.
e) Her husband works in a church. She teaches religion. She is very kind.
f) She is a really good friend. She laughs a lot. She has a beautiful smile.

2 What happens to the following characters at the end of the story?

a) Matthew ....
b) Gilbert ....
c) Anne ....

After Reading

3 **What are the characters like? Tick (✓) the correct adjective and write examples.**

Anne

kind ✓ funny ✓
helpful ✓
friendly ✓
enthusiastic ✓

Examples: Anne helps Marilla at the end of the book. Anne speaks to Aunt Josephine when Diana is in trouble…

Matthew

kind ☐ funny ☐
helpful ☐
friendly ☐
enthusiastic ☐

Examples: ....
....
....
....
....

Marilla

kind ☐ funny ☐
helpful ☐
friendly ☐
enthusiastic ☐

Examples: ....
....
....
....
....

4 **Work with a friend. Ask and answer questions together.**

What are you like?

I am enthusiastic because…

Diana

kind ☐ funny ☐
helpful ☐
friendly ☐
enthusiastic ☐

Examples: ....
....
....
....
....

Mrs Rachel

kind ☐ funny ☐
helpful ☐
friendly ☐
enthusiastic ☐

Examples: ....
....
....
....
....

65

After Reading

Plot and Theme

1 The following are important themes in the story. Match the themes to the actions.

a) ☐ Friendship   b) ☐ Saying sorry
c) ☐ Being hard-working   d) ☐ Growing up

1. Gilbert tells Anne that he is sorry for making jokes about her hair.
2. Anne tells Aunt Josephine not to punish Diana for jumping on the bed.
3. Anne tells Matthew and Marilla that she did well in her exam.
4. Gilbert and Anne learn to work together and forgive each other.

2 Look at the pictures and write the correct theme from Exercise 1.

After Reading

3 Put the events from the story in the correct order.

a) ☐ Anne and Gilbert are 'equal firsts' in the exam.

b) ☐ Anne recites a poem at a concert.

c) ☐ Mrs Rachel makes a dress for Anne.

d) ☐ Matthew starts to have heart problems.

e) ☐ Marilla cuts Anne's hair.

f) ☐ Diana thinks Anne is dead.

g) ☐ Anne thinks she has poisoned Mrs Allan.

h) ☐ Matthew dies.

i) ☐ Marilla cries and Anne goes away to school.

j) ☐ Gilbert tries to make friends with Anne.

k) ☐ Diana invites Anne to her house for a sleepover.

l) ☐ Miss Stacy selects students for a special class.

m) ☐ Matthew and Marilla lose all their money.

n) ☐ Anne changes her plans and stays at Avonlea.

4 Choose one of the events in Exercise 3. With a partner, talk about how the characters felt.

5 Match the details with the correct chapter title.

a) ☐ Hair trouble

b) ☐ A boating accident

c) ☐ The big exam

d) ☐ The concert

e) ☐ A dream comes true

1 Anne stays at Aunt Josephine's house.

2 Matthew begins to feel unwell.

3 Anne pretends to be a famous character from a poem.

4 Gilbert thinks Anne is beautiful.

5 Anne buys hair colour from a travelling salesman.

After Reading

Language

1 Complete the sentences with these words in the story.

> rivals   shop assistant   scholarship   sleepover   timetable   cold

a) Tomorrow is Diana's birthday. She's invited me to her house for a ....

b) She had a .... and did not feel very well.

c) The next day Matthew went to buy a dress for Anne. The .... was a very pretty young woman.

d) The two of them were open .... in school now. They were always competing.

e) Anne met lots of new students and professors and received her .... for classes.

f) The .... was for the student with the highest score in English. This was one thousand dollars for college fees.

2 Past simple or present perfect? Circle the correct form of the verbs.

a) Matthew and Marilla soon began / have begun to like Anne's strange ways and affectionate character.

b) Over the following year Anne became / has become best friends with a girl called Diana.

c) Tomorrow is Diana's birthday. She invited / has invited me to her house for a sleepover.

d) You didn't do / haven't done anything strange for more than two months.

e) She had a cold but she felt / has felt better after the cake went in the oven.

After Reading

K 3 Read the text about Anne and Gilbert. Choose the best word/s, 1, 2 or 3, to complete the text.

Anne and Gilbert were in competition **(a)** .... each other. They saw each other but didn't speak. It was like they were **(b)** .... Anne secretly wished that she was friends with Gilbert again. But **(c)** .... also wanted to get a higher score than him in the exam. Everyone thought Gilbert was going to get **(d)** .... score. She wanted to make Matthew and Marilla proud. The results were late. Finally after three weeks of waiting, they **(e)** .... Diana came running to the house with a newspaper. Matthew was working and Mrs Rachel was talking to Marilla. 'Matthew, I **(f)** .... I'm first. Well, one of the first,' said Anne.

a) **1** with   **2** for   **3** at
b) **1** foreigners **2** strangers   **3** friends
c) **1** her   **2** he   **3** she
d) **1** the biggest **2** the highest **3** most high
e) **1** have arrived **2** arrived   **3** should arrive
f) **1** pass   **2** 've passed   **3** has passed

After Reading

Exit Test

1 **Listen to the extracts. For each question, choose the right answer (1, 2 or 3).**

a) Where was Anne?
   1 ☐ on land
   2 ☐ in the water
   3 ☐ on a platform

b) What did Anne think?
   1 ☐ She was in trouble.
   2 ☐ She was able to read.
   3 ☐ She was late.

c) What was the cake like?
   1 ☐ very good
   2 ☐ horrible
   3 ☐ nothing special

d) Why is Anne silent?
   1 ☐ She is tired.
   2 ☐ She likes thinking.
   3 ☐ She hates school.

e) How did Anne feel?
   1 ☐ She missed home.
   2 ☐ She hated the Academy.
   3 ☐ She was lovesick.

After Reading

 2 Listen and tick (✓) the correct picture.

a) 1  2 ☐

b) 1 ☐  2 ☐

c) 1  2 ☐

d) 1  2 ☐

71

After Reading

Project

CANADIAN 🍁 FACT FILE

WEB Create a fact file about Canada and Prince Edward Island, where *Anne of Green Gables* is set. Use the Internet to help you find ideas and photos.

a) Work in groups of four.
b) Consider these things:
- Flag
- Official languages
- Climate
- Nature
- Geography
- People and culture
- Government and economy
- History

c) Put together your fact file and present it to the class.